MR MEN
The Big Bump

Roger Hargreaves

In these stories you will meet:

Mr Bump

Mr Messy

And these more difficult words:

house   garden

EGMONT
We bring stories to life

Book Band: Red

MR. MEN   **LITTLE MISS**

MR. MEN™ LITTLE MISS™ © THOIP (a SANRIO company)

The Big Bump © 2016 THOIP (a SANRIO company)
Printed and published under licence from Price Stern Sloan, Inc., Los Angeles.
Published in Great Britain by Egmont UK Limited
The Yellow Building, 1 Nicholas Road, London, W11 4AN

ISBN 978 1 4052 8266 6
63467/1
Printed in Singapore

Illustrated by Adam Hargreaves
Series and book banding consultant: Nikki Gamble

Written by Jane Riordan
Designed by Cassie Benjamin

MIX
Paper
FSC   FSC® C018306

The Big Bump

This is Mr Bump.

Hello, Mr Bump.

Crash!

Mr Bump has bumps.

Crash!
Lots of bumps.

Bump!
Lots and lots of bumps.

Mr Bump went out.

Bump went Mr Bump.

Splat went the eggs!
Splat! Splat! Splat!

Bump went Mr Bump.
Splash went the paint!
Splash!
Splash!
Splash!

What a mess!
Goodbye, Mr Bump!

23

Mr Messy in the Snow

This is Mr Messy.

Hello, Mr Messy.

Mr Messy is messy.

His house is messy.

His garden is messy.

Then snow fell.

Mr Messy's garden
was not messy.

Mr Messy went to
his shed.

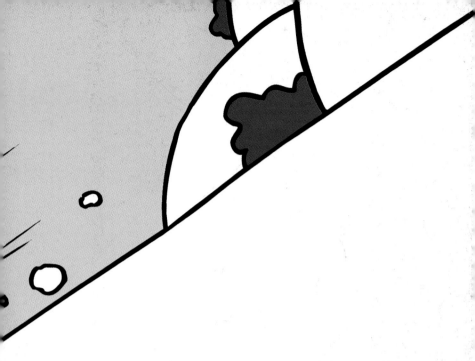

The snow was fun.
Whoosh!

Stamp! Stamp! Stamp!

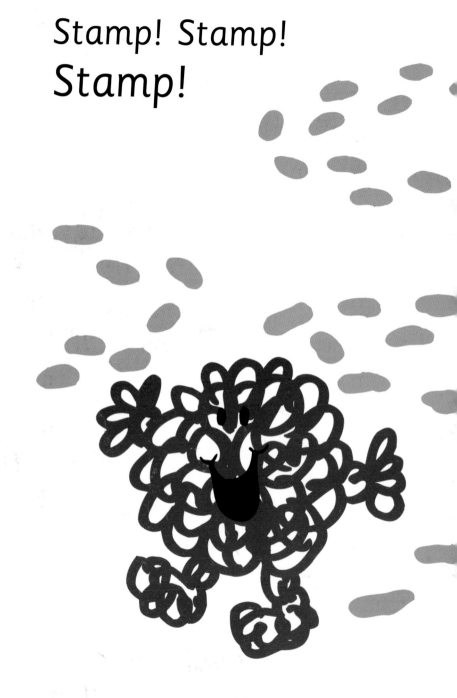

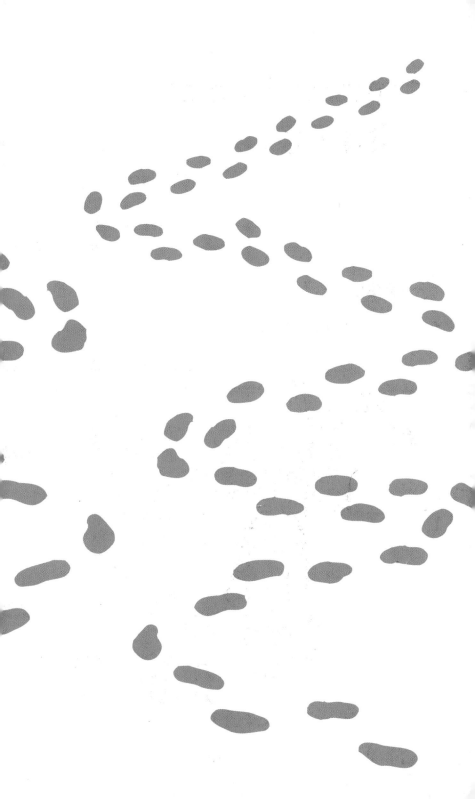

42

Lots and lots of fun.

Mr Messy is glad to
have a messy garden!

Goodbye,
Mr Messy!

Messy Mix-up

Follow the lines to match Mr Bump to the words beginning with a 'b' sound and Mr Messy to the words beginning with an 'm' sound.

Sh! Sh! Sh!

These words all end with a 'sh' sound. Read the words and then match up the words with the pictures.

Crash!

Whoosh!

Splash!

Can you think of any other words that end with a 'sh' sound?